The Country Mouse and The City Mouse

A Tale of Tolerance

Retold by Karen Jennings and Mark Pierce
Illustrated by Dennis Hockerman

Famous Fables

Reader's Digest Young Families

Emma, a humble country mouse, beamed with pride at her vegetable garden.

"I must invite my cousin Henry from the city to join me for a grand harvest feast," she exclaimed. Emma sat down at her desk and wrote her cousin a letter.

A week later, there was a knock at the door.

"Hello, cousin!" said Henry with a big smile. "Thanks ever so much for inviting me. It's nice to be away from all the hub-bub of the city."

"You must be hungry after your journey," Emma said. "Dinner's coming right up."

"My four favorite words," said Henry, licking his lips.

Emma set down large steaming bowls of freshly cooked vegetables on the table. The two mice cousins enjoyed a delicious meal.

"Thank you, Emma," said Henry. "That was a splendid
meal. Now, what's for dessert?"

"Dessert? Oh, no!" Emma exclaimed. "I meant to
pick a big basket of fresh berries, but then I started
cooking and forgot all about dessert." Emma looked
around her kitchen frantically for something to serve.

"Why don't I run to the corner store and get us something sweet?" Henry asked.

"The what?" Emma gazed at him curiously.

"The corner store. Don't tell me you don't have a corner store?"

"No, cousin," Emma giggled. "Here in the country we grow all our food."

"I couldn't do that. The only thing I would grow is *hungry*," said Henry.

"I should have brought something from the city," said Henry. "We have the most wonderful desserts you've ever tasted." Henry jumped up. "I know. Why don't you come with me into the city for dessert?"

"Really?" Emma asked.

"Really," Henry replied.

When the two travelers reached the city, Emma looked around at all the amazing sights. The buildings were so tall they blocked the sky from view. Cars and trucks raced about blaring their horns. People were in a terrific rush.

"What a busy place the city is," Emma remarked.

"Yes, isn't it great?" Henry said. "Hang on, we'll be at my townhouse soon."

"This is my home, cousin," Henry said.

"Oh, Henry, it's glorious," Emma said looking at his stately building.

"And that is where we'll get our dessert," Henry said. "It's called Sweet Treats. No one is there now because it is so late. Let's go."

Emma and Henry scurried under the front door of Sweet Treats and ran to the kitchen.

"Dessert!" Henry said, pointing to the cart that towered over them.

They ran up the tablecloth and onto the dessert cart.

The cart was filled with the most colorful, fancy foods Emma had ever seen. There were layer cakes, cupcakes, chocolate éclairs, cheesecakes and pies of all kinds.

"There," Henry declared. "That was worth the climb, wasn't it?"

Emma nodded. She was dizzy with delight. The two mice sat down and began nibbling away.

Suddenly, they heard a loud "*Meeeeow!*"

"That's the cook's cat, Pierre. We'd better run before he catches us in here," said Henry.

They scrambled to the floor, but there was Pierre—waiting for them.

"We have to make a run for it," yelled Henry.

As Emma and Henry tried to dash out, Pierre's paw landed on Emma's tail. She was trapped.

"Help!" cried Emma. Henry grabbed the cat's whiskers. Pierre yowled. He lifted his paw to swipe at Henry, and Emma was free!

Henry let go of Pierre's whiskers, and the two mice slid under the back door into the yard.

"Once we get across the yard, we're home," Henry whispered as he pointed to a large, snoring dog. "That's Rufus. He doesn't like mice." Slowly they tiptoed past Rufus. But Rufus opened his eyes and growled at Emma and Henry.

"Come on, cousin. Hurry!" Henry said. The two mice dashed to the house as Rufus bounded after them.

Safe inside, Henry smiled and said, "So, wasn't that the most heavenly dessert you ever tasted?"

"Yes, cousin, but was it worth all that danger?" Emma replied. "The city life is exciting, but it isn't for me. I prefer the country where a mouse can eat in peace."

"I understand," Henry said. "The city is not for everyone, but I love it."

"Do promise me, dear Henry," Emma said, "that you will come to my house next autumn."

"Of course I will, Emma. And next time, I'll bring the dessert! Now, I'll take you home."

The next evening while cousin Henry went out for a night of dancing in the big city, Emma settled in for a homemade meal of turnip and cabbage stew, followed by a nice quiet cup of tea. "Ah," she sighed, "there's nothing like the country."

Famous Fables, Lasting Virtues

Tips for Parents

Now that you've read The Country Mouse and The City Mouse, *use these pages as a guide in teaching your child the virtues in the story. By talking about the story and its message and engaging in the suggested activities, you can help your child develop good judgment and a strong moral character.*

About Tolerance

When children learn to respect and tolerate differences in other people, they are learning to appreciate and get along well with others—lessons that will help them all through their lives. Here are a few strategies you can use:

1. *Show by example.* Parents are powerful role models, and kids absorb what their parents say even when parents think their children aren't listening. Be sensitive to your own attitudes, even statements that appear harmless, such as "City folks are crazy drivers."

2. *Broaden your child's world.* Seek out opportunities for your child to play and interact with different types of kids. Participate in community-based activities—such as sports teams, scouting groups, and volunteer groups—or activities sponsored by your place of worship.

3. *Be selective about books and media.* Read books that show people of different backgrounds and cultures. Watch videos and TV shows with your child and discuss issues or stereotypes.

Talking Time

After reading *The Country Mouse and The City Mouse*, talk to your child about the issues raised in the story. You can also talk about these issues as you are reading the story together. Here are some suggestions to get you started:

✦ What present did Cousin Henry bring to Emma? Do you think Emma had ever seen such a thing? What else would have made an unusual gift?